The Ticking Box

Mark Cowling

ISBN: **1505663253**
ISBN-13: 978-1505663259

DEDICATION

To my wife Rachel

CONTENTS

Acknowledgments i

1 Discovering the adventure 1

2 Discovering the Ticking Box 13

3 Discovering Adam 26

4 Discovering Joseph 44

5 Discovering Daniel 59

6 Discovering Jesus 70

7 Discovering Herth 87

ACKNOWLEDGMENTS

Thanks to Evee Lees for the illustrations, Tom for showing me the power of pictures, Sam and Cath for proof reading, Rachel for always encouraging me and of course our children who inspire me!

1. DISCOVERING THE ADVENTURE

Emily Grace was nine years old and lived at number nine Coalpit Close on the edge of an ordinary town in the north of England. This story is about a most surprising and incredible adventure she had that made her realise there is so much more to this world than she had ever realised. You might find it hard to believe but it all started when Emily discovered that an extremely tall tower, made of thousands of red bricks, had magical powers to talk to her. Quite a few tall brick chimneys were still dotted across the town, from the old days when textiles were made there, woven by steam powered machines to make clothes. Those chimneys were not used now but they still stood there, still and quiet. One of those chimneys cast its shadow over Emily's house, and Emily

would often stare at it from her bedroom window. Emily's tower, for that's what she called it, was so tall that on a grey day, which was quite often, it looked like it was actually touching the clouds. It was so tall that she had wondered, if it were to fall over on a windy day, whether it might come crashing down through her window. But Emily wasn't scared of her tower, in fact she rather loved it. She loved how the sides from its hexagonal shape were always different colours in the daylight. And she loved how sparrow hawks would land on a branch that was growing out of one of the sides of the tower, like a bit of scruffy stubble from an old man's chin. Emily thought it was amazing that anything could stay settled in one place for so many years. That wasn't her story. She had moved house five times so far and nothing seemed to stand still in her life. But one thing Emily did feel she had in common with her tower was that it stuck out a lot. It was different from everything else around it. And if you asked Emily what the hardest thing was for her, she probably would have said it was trying to fit in. She was different. She hadn't come up from nursery school with everyone because she had only just moved into the area, she spoke with a slightly different accent, and most of all, she just saw things differently. Oh, and her parents were a bit different too. They were always giving their things away to homeless people and often bought things for their house from the second hand shop. Emily believed they were like this because they had lived in Africa once and somehow that had changed them. Whatever it was, it meant Emily was the last to get the latest gadget or new phone and she felt this didn't help her fit in either. And when you feel you don't fit in, you know you have to be brave everyday because others will tease you.

When Emily Grace got up in the morning to go to school, she would put on her uniform that sat neatly laid out on the chair in front of her desk. Then she would pick up her hairbrush and brush out all the tangles and knots in her hair that somehow got there when she was asleep. Often whilst she was doing this, which took a few minutes, Emily would stand at her bedroom window and look at her tower that stood so straight and strong and never looked tired or sleepy as Emily often felt when she woke up in the winter mornings.

It was a particularly grey winter morning when, to Emily's surprise, she was sure that her tower spoke to her... Perhaps "communicate a message," would be a better way to explain it. The tower seemed to have words, very large words in fact, engraved down the length of it, as if written by a giant. The words were on each of the flat sides of the hexagonal tower and seemed to glow and it was very odd to see. What was perhaps more odd, but amazing, was that the tower seemed to spin round so that Emily could read the words . The words read “Press,” then on the next face, “Receive,” then on the next face “Button,” and then on the next face “Princess Clock.” It all happened so quickly, and in the middle of trying to pull her brush through a particularly stubborn knot in

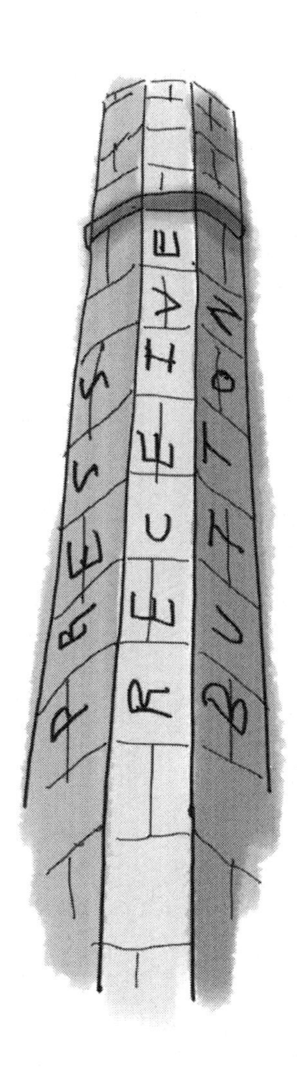

her hair, that she thought she must be imagining it. What's more, Emily's mum was now calling up the stairs for the third time:

"Hurry up Emily! Get in the car immediately please! We're running late for school!" The school doors were locked at five minutes to nine which made running late extra stressful. None of them wanted to take the walk of shame through the school office, so other than gaze for a moment at a now blank tower, Emily didn't think any more about what the words meant. She just took a deep breath to face another school day and ran downstairs and off to school.

It wasn't until that evening that she began to think about it again. Emily's Dad had finished reading her a story, kissed Emily good night and went downstairs to get on with some work as usual. He always seemed to be working but even so, Emily knew her family weren't very well off. Emily rolled over in bed and looked at her Princess clock. At that moment she could see in her mind the words that she believed she had seen on the tower that morning whilst she had been brushing her hair: "Press," "Receive," "Button," and "Princess Clock." Emily's first thought was not how strange it was that the tower spoke to her but one of being puzzled that she had never seen a "Receive," button on her clock before. She picked up the clock and spun it around in her hand. To her

amazement there was a button, a small black plastic button, which she had never noticed before. It was switched up and underneath the button moulded into the pink plastic it said “Receive.” If you would like to know what happened when Emily switched the button down, read on.

Switch the button to the “Receive,” position is exactly what Emily did. Nothing happened. That is, until Emily put the clock back down on her bedside table. Then something most definitely did happen. First, the clock bleeped three sharp little beeps. Then she could hardly believe her eyes! The sides of the clock seemed to spin over as if on little hinges. One at a time they appeared to flip over. The top panel, the first side panel, the second side panel, then the front panel, where the hands were, disappeared as it flipped over. Then the back panel flipped and finally the whole clock, or whatever it was now, fell backwards and the bottom panel flipped over. The whole clock had turned itself inside out and now the clock was not a clock but a small box with a rather strange pattern on it! As Emily looked a little closer at the box that was her clock, she saw that it looked like a strange kind of map. The map was mostly a grey-black sort of a colour and it had a line on it that seemed to go all around the box. She reached out a hand towards the clock box and then bravely picked it up. As she drew the box nearer to her, she could still hear the gentle tick tick ticking of the clock, even though the hands of her clock had disappeared. Emily studied the pattern of the box and then ran her finger over the line which was a dark red colour. The line was slightly raised up and even though her room was dark, she was able to run her finger along the line quite easily. She followed it from what appeared to be the start of the line on one of the faces, all the way until she had run her finger around all the faces of the clock box. As her finger reached the end of the line the strangest thing happened. Can you guess what?

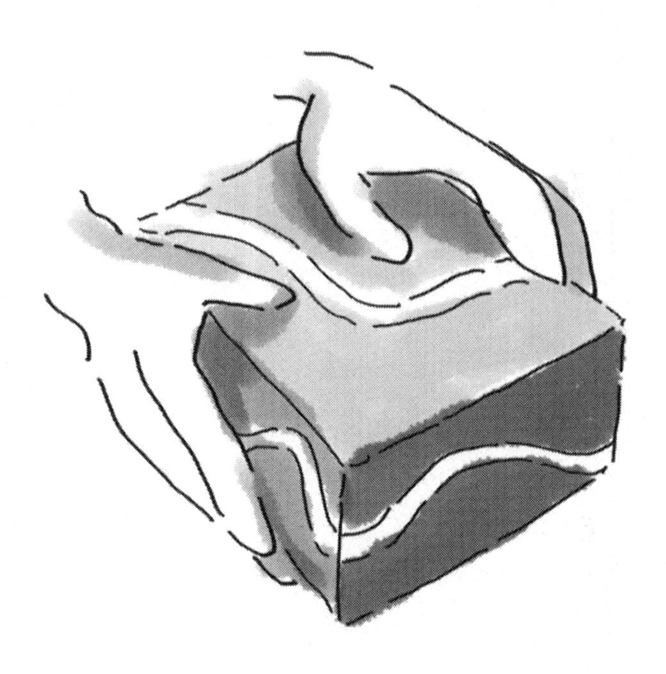

The box in Emily's hands began to move! Not only did the clock move but Emily began to move with it! It was as though some invisible carpet was carrying them both. As the clock box rose up in the air, so did

Emily Grace! Emily's pink flowery duvet fell off from around her legs as she rose up and floated up in mid-air. You might think that Emily would have let go in panic, but she didn't. She felt very calm about what was happening and, in fact, she was curious about what was happening. Emily had always been a curious girl. Ever since she was a baby, she had always asked questions about why things were the way they were and always looked to see how things worked, sometimes getting into quite uncomfortable positions in the process of finding out. This occasion was no exception. Emily's curiosity was stronger than any concern about what might happen. And so, with her hands still around the clock box and floating in mid-air, she waited to see what would happen next. What happened next is even more amazing than anything we have heard so far! Would you like to know what did happen?

Just as Emily was realising that something very strange indeed was happening, the clock seemed to lead itself, and Emily, in mid-air, out of the bedroom, across the landing and into the bathroom. There, in the bathroom behind the toilet, the square window was wide open which surprised Emily because it wasn't open when she had brushed her teeth half an hour ago. The clock headed straight for the window and Emily with it and, before she knew it, Emily was floating up over the roof of her house! The garden already looked quite small from such a height

and she clasped her hands around the clock just a bit more firmly not wanting to tumble down to the ground now she was so high. As she looked up she could see the clock was making its way towards the chimney, right up to the very top of her tower! It was dark now and she thought her tower seemed to be glowing as she travelled towards it, as though again it was speaking to her, asking her to come closer. It wasn't very long, a minute or so, before she was floating over the top of her tower. This, thought Emily, is what it must be like to be the sparrow hawk which lands on the branch that grows out of one of the sides of the tower, like a bit of scruffy stubble from an old man's chin. Just as she was thinking this thought, something a little bit scary happened. The clock, with Emily following it, suddenly dropped down the hole in the top of the chimney tower and into pitch blackness! She couldn't see a thing now. All she knew was she was falling at quite a speed, because she could feel the air rushing past her. Down and down and down she went. Where would it all end? If you would like to know the answer, read on.

2. DISCOVERING THE TICKING BOX

Emily was falling down and down and down and couldn't see a thing. It had seemed like five minutes or more of this falling and Emily was beginning to feel trapped. Just as she wondered about letting go of this clock box, she found herself being shot out of the tunnel she had been in. Now she could not believe her eyes. Emily Grace was in space! All around her were stars sparkling in the blackness of space. As she looked over her shoulder, she could see the world where she had come from and where she lived right behind her. It was getting smaller and smaller, just like her own house had done, as she travelled onwards and onwards. Emily thought she must be travelling very fast indeed, and yet her hair

was only gently blowing which made her feel like she couldn't have been travelling very fast. She began to wonder where all this might end, or even if there could be an end. After all, space is a big place, and she could be travelling forever. It was so beautiful though, and Emily didn't think she could imagine anything more beautiful. The stars looked like jewellery in the dark enormous skies of space and she could see the moon looming brightly in the distance. When she looked at herself, tiny in all this space, she felt so privileged to be sitting there, at that moment, and wished it would never end.

As Emily was thinking this she noticed that now all the stars and the planets had disappeared, and instead it was just a pure blackness of space. But out in the distance there seemed to be a small object that was getting gradually bigger. Bigger and bigger it looked until Emily could see it clearly right in front of her. It was another box, a cube shaped box. It was not very big, in fact it looked as though you could pick it up. It probably was not much bigger than the big plastic toy box in Emily's house. The box had two hand prints on it, one on each side of the box. They were coloured red and were sunk into the box, so that you could snugly fit your hands into each of the hand prints. Then, on one of the other sides of this box in space was a dial. The dial was quite large and made out of bronze metal. And on the dial were two arrows, facing in opposite directions. One facing up and one facing down. The box was making a sound. It was ticking. Tick, tick, tick, tick it went. Over and over and over again, it ticked with a deep sound. Tick, tick, tick, tick.

Then a kind voice spoke up, "You can put your clock box down on top of the Ticking Box and then your hands will be free to discover one of the greatest secrets." Emily followed the kind voice's instructions.

The voice was a nice voice, a gentle man's voice, that reminded Emily of her Grandad who she had loved very much but now missed very much since he had died. As Emily listened, she heard the kind voice saying her name.

"Emily,"

"Yes?"

"I am so glad you have made this trip. You're a clever girl, working out the secret steps you needed to make in order for this trip to happen."

The voice continued, “I am so glad you have made this trip because there is a great adventure that awaits you.” Emily pondered the idea of an adventure awaiting her that could be better than the adventure she had already experienced, travelling out here into space. Then her mind turned to practicalities and she spoke up.

“Will I have enough time for this adventure?” she asked tentatively. “Oh yes,” replied the kind voice. “All the time in the world. All the time in time.” Emily didn’t quite understand what the kind voice meant by “all the time in time,” but she simply replied,

“Oh good.” And with that, the kind voice spoke some more. “Emily, this is the Ticking Box. Not your clock box, but THE Ticking Box. You are the only person in the world to have ever seen the Ticking Box and nobody else in the world knows that it exists.” “Why is it ticking?” asked Emily. “It’s not a bomb is it?”

“That’s a very good question Emily,” said the kind voice. “It is ticking because it has always been ticking. Before all this that you have seen around you, the stars and the moon and the earth, before all of this was here, the Ticking Box was ticking.”

“Is the Ticking Box immortal?” asked Emily. “I mean can it live forever?”

“Another brilliant question Emily,” replied the kind voice. “I believe it is and I believe it can.”

“Wow!” said Emily, thinking that made the Ticking Box very old indeed, even older than her tower. This made her wonder what the Ticking Box might have experienced or seen in that very large amount of time.

“And what about the hand prints and the dial?” asked Emily curiously. “The answer to that question is the secret that is most amazing about the Ticking Box,” said the kind voice. “When you push the dial upwards or downwards and then put your hands onto the two red hand prints on each side of the box, you will suddenly find that the box starts moving forwards or backwards.”

“That’s incredible!” said Emily

“But what’s more incredible is that the Ticking Box cannot only move forwards and backwards in space, but it can move forwards and backwards in time,” Emily’s eyes widened in amazement. “That means if you twist and turn the dial forwards and you hold onto the box, you will start travelling into the future, into a time that has not happened yet.

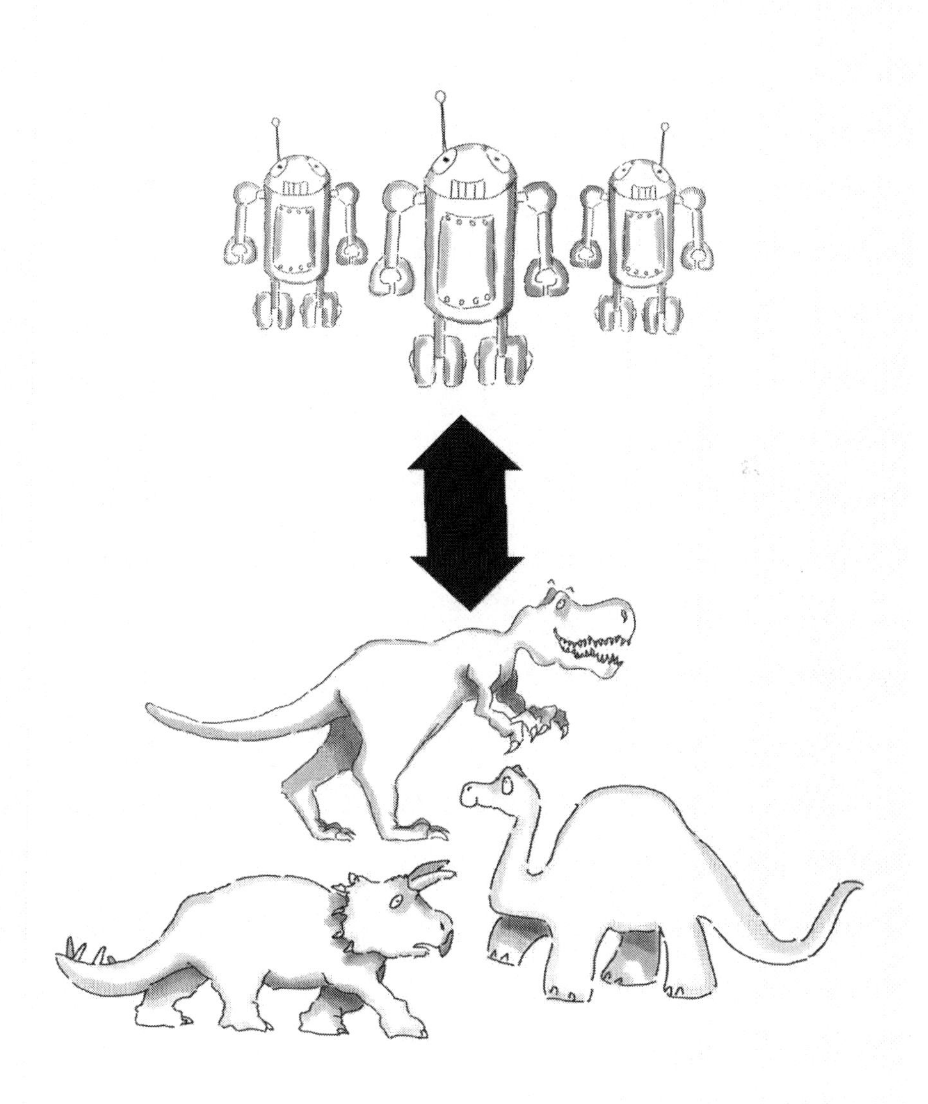

The more you turn the dial, the further into the future you will travel, one year, two years, five years, 500 years, maybe even more. Similarly, when you turn the dial backwards, you start travelling back in time, one year, two years and so on… Do you get the idea?"

"Yes," said Emily, running her hand gently along the top of the Ticking Box as though it were a shiny new car. "So when you go back in time, you go back in history to things that have already happened. Like last year's birthday or the day you were born or when your granddad was born or when dinosaurs roamed the earth or anything like that I suppose."

"That is the most special secret of the Ticking Box," said the kind voice. "And you, Emily, are invited to take a trip with the Ticking Box. But think carefully, because you only get one chance."

"Amazing!" whispered Emily and her eyes grew bigger and bigger as the possibilities began to dawn on her, and that meeting the Ticking Box was only the beginning of her adventure. "How does it work?" she asked.

The kind voice explained that it worked using electro-magnetic waves, just like the ones that connect a phone to the internet. "There is a metal ball inside the Ticking Box that is made up of lots of spheres, like layers of an onion, which can all move in different directions. When you turn the dial and hold on to the hand prints on the side of the box, the spheres make patterns of electro-magnetic waves and sends them out into space. Those patterns are able to open up tunnels in space called "wormholes" which you can travel along. They can take you anywhere you want, so long as the Ticking Box agrees to it."

Emily thought that the Ticking Box was going to be much better than the phone she had wanted for so long. She started to think what fun it would

be to race past all the planets and see for herself their beautiful colours which she had only ever read about in school books. She realised she could be a pioneer, someone who was the first in the world to do the things that the Ticking Box could enable her to do. After all, so far the most famous spaceman was Neil Armstrong who had stepped foot on the moon. Emily thought she could probably go a lot further and do a lot more than that. That would make her famous! She would be on every TV channel in the world. Maybe like other superstars, Emily's fame would be so great she could sell perfume with her name on it or T-shirts with her face on them! Not only would she be famous, but she would be rich. People would probably pay her lots of money too and she could finally choose her own house rather than living in other people's houses which Emily's family rented and which she never really felt at home in. She would choose all the colours of everything, especially the carpets which would be soft and cosy rather than thin and cold. With a mixture of feelings of quiet excitement and disbelief, Emily moved her hand towards the bronze looking dial as she began to think about turning the dial to start moving. As she did so she realised she hadn't given much thought to moving forward or back through time. That was such an amazing possibility that Emily didn't know what to think. But Emily did think, and she thought she should give it some time before she decided

what to do and where to go on the adventure that laid before her. One thing Emily didn't consider was how to get home. It didn't seem important at this moment. Instead, she held on to the Ticking Box looking at its every detail, like you do to a new present when you unwrap it. As she allowed her mind to imagine what would be the best adventure to take, Emily started to think about what her school friends would most like to hear about. Emily went to a school called St. Peter's Primary School which she liked. They had assemblies in the morning after the register was taken and usually someone would come and speak to them about something interesting they had done or perhaps read a Bible story. Emily was thinking how nice it would be to tell all her friends in assembly about what the planets, like Saturn and Mars and Neptune, looked like when another thought started to grow. What about the time travel option? How amazing that would be to tell people about seeing our horrible histories or maybe the worryingly unknown future. I think, thought Emily, one should start from the beginning. And she began to think about what she knew about the beginnings. "Well, it all started with cells I suppose," said Emily out loud and then realising that it didn't really matter if she spoke out loud and that in fact it helped her think clearly, she carried on. "Of course those cells grew up and we got dinosaurs and then people." She took a deep breath and carried on, "I'm not sure I'm brave enough to visit the dinosaurs, but I would like to visit..." She paused as she thought about the Bible story from her assembly last week about the first people. "I would like to visit Adam and Eve in the Garden of Eden… now *that* would be something to tell everybody at school!" She looked down at her hands and asked, "How do we get there then?"

The kind voice explained to Emily how to turn the bronze dial backwards until it said stop and then to put her hands in the red handprints on the side of the Ticking Box. Before Emily knew it she was moving. It felt a bit like travelling through the tunnel of a whirlwind although a bit calmer. And, after what seemed like only half a minute, the end of the tunnel appeared and Emily walked out. She had travelled through space and time! If you'd like to know what Emily saw, read on.

3. DISCOVERING ADAM

Emily found herself in a beautiful walled garden. There was a path into the garden and lots of beautiful shrubs and plants and trees that had been looked after. She let go of the Ticking Box and it gently came to rest on the path she was standing on. Then she began to follow the path. There was a stone carving of two swans that made a ball shape and a gentle fountain of water coming out from the middle that made that nice relaxing water splashing sound. And there were people in the garden, of all ages, enjoying the garden and playing. Emily decided to be brave and walked up to a young girl sunbathing on the grass who seemed to be chewing gum.

“Hello,” said Emily.

“Hello,” said the girl. She blew a bubble until it burst and then carried on chewing.

“My name is Emily. What’s yours?”

“Jessica,” said the girl. “Are you having a nice day?”

“Yes,” said Emily looking into Jessica’s pretty brown eyes, “A lovely day thanks. I’m err... looking for Adam and Eve.”

“Oh yes,” said Jessica, “you’ll find Adam digging on the vegetable patch over there,” and Jessica sat up and pointed down the garden.

“Thank you Jessica,” and Emily began to walk on as Jessica blew another bubble. As it burst, Jessica called out,

“Adam’s lovely but he’s a bit stressy at the moment!” Emily looked back and smiled, wondering what on earth that meant, but carried on to search for Adam on his vegetable patch.

Emily walked down the lawn until she reached a great set of stone steps. As she looked down to the next terrace of the garden she could see a wheel barrow in front of some bushes. That looks promising, thought Emily, and she skipped down the steps.

She reached the wheel barrow and walked around it following the path between the tall bushy trees when, to her surprise, a large bird swooped down and brushed her head with the underside of its wing. Emily was confident with animals but it did make her step back and wonder why the bird had got so close. She watched it glide upwards and away. It was a rose pink colour and looked a bit like a Parrot.

The garden opened up in front of her with a good number of long flower beds that looked neatly kept and raked. Over in the corner was a man holding a hoe and rubbing it down with a flat stone. Emily walked over and called out: “Hello!”

The man looked up and smiled. “Hi,” he said and carried on rubbing down his hoe whilst chewing his gum. Emily could see the bird had settled nearby, perched on a spade handle which was wedged into the soft soil of a well dug flower bed.

“I’m Emily,” said Emily with a smile.

“Hello Emily, I don’t recognise you. Who are you?”

“I’m a visitor,” she said thinking quickly.

“Oh yeah, where are you visiting from then?”

“Oh...” Emily wondered where to begin, “Visiting from a place that seems like another world from here.”

“Oh,” said the man. “Well this place is pretty special I suppose, even if it’s not what it was.”

“Are you Adam?” asked Emily.

“Yes, I am Adam,” and he smiled gently.

"And are you married to Eve?"

"Yes, indeed I am."

"But I thought you were supposed to be the first people on earth?"

"No, not the first people exactly but certainly the first 'newmans.'"

"Humans did you say?" questioned Emily.

"No, newmans," repeated Adam.

"What's a newman?" asked Emily frowning with confusion.

“A newman is one of these,” said Adam, lifting his shirt up and showing his tummy. The bird which was watching flapped his wings and ruffled his feathers. Emily immediately noticed there was something different about Adam’s tummy. Can you guess what?

What was different about Adam’s tummy was he didn’t have a belly button! Suddenly, it dawned on Emily, that the first people can hardly have been born from people otherwise they wouldn't be first. She remembered her school assembly Bible story that said God made Adam and Eve from the dust. "So you're like a new breed of people?" suggested Emily.

"You could say that," replied Adam.

"So what's different about you to the other people here?" enquired Emily. "Have you worked that out?"

"Oh yes," said Adam. "We can hear God talking."

"Really?" said Emily, her eyes widening. "What does God sound like?"

"He sounds just like us when he speaks." The bird squawked and turned around on the spade handle to turn its back on them as if disapproving of their conversation.

"That's amazing!" said Emily, wondering what God might speak about.

"Yes, it is good Emily. But we found that privilege comes with a responsibility too." As he said that, he blew a big bubble that burst covering most of his face. He peeled it off him and pushed it back into his mouth and carried on chewing.

"That was a big bubble!" remarked Emily.

"Yeah, not bad hey?"

"My brothers love Bubble Gum," said Emily.

"Bubble Gum! Huh? That's what you call it hey? Neat name I must say."

"Yes, we call it Bubble Gum, what do you call it?" asked Emily

"We call it chew," answered Adam. "Cos that's all it's good for, but I like your name better cos we can't stop blowing bubbles with it." He handed Emily a block of white chew. "Give it a go and tell me if it's as good as your bubble gum." Emily put the chew in her mouth wondering why Adam hadn't at least called it Bubble Chew. It was softer than what she was used to and it crackled like stardust at first and then it tasted of pineapple.

"Different!" she said chewing.

"Want to have a bubble competition?" asked Adam

"Definitely."

"OK, you go first," said Adam. Emily gave her gum a rapid chew and then gave it her best go. She pushed her tongue into the chew and a small golf ball size bubble appeared and then popped. "Well done!" said Adam trying to be encouraging.

"No good!" said Emily.

"It's the first bubble that counts!" said Adam. "Now, let me try." Adam got a good, steadily growing bubble started which slowly got bigger and bigger – about as big as his head. Then he seemed to stop and Emily wondered what he was doing. Then, to her immense surprise, she could see Adam was forming another bubble, this time inside the first bubble. The second bubble gradually got larger until it began to start pushing the first bubble out. "That's clever!" thought Emily to herself. Now Adam's bubble was really big. As big as a large beach ball that Emily had on her last beach holiday. Adam put his arms out and made a bow and the suddenly it burst, covering his entire face and most of his head. He looked like an alien for a minute until he peeled it off in one swipe and pushed it back into his mouth. Emily clapped.

"Well done!" she exclaimed. "Never seen anything like it!"

"Why, thank you, Emily," replied Adam. "Bit of a party trick I've been practising."

"Jessica said you were a bit stressed," said Emily "but I don't see it with you making bubble gum bubbles like that."

"Well... things haven't gone very well for Eve and I just recently."

"Oh, I'm sorry," said Emily, wondering what that could mean.

"Yeah, I'm sorry too. Right now we're having real trouble getting things to grow in this garden."

"Oh…But it's so beautiful."

"I'm afraid it's dying," said Adam. "It's the food that's been affected first, but we're seeing signs of everything beginning to die." Adam pulled at the bark of a fruit tree growing in one of the flower beds. A strip came off in his hand and he peered down at it apparently confirming his fears.

"That's terrible!" Emily frowned again. "What's the problem?" Adam screwed his face up and then replied,

"We just couldn't stop ourselves,"

"From what?" said Emily concerned.

"Do you ever have times," continued Adam, "when you just really want something? You want it so bad you can't think of anything else?" "Oh dear," said Emily sympathetically, wondering what that meant. "Well," said Adam, "We knew God had said that we should not eat the nuts that fall from the Bubba tree, but once you started touching them it was almost impossible to stop ourselves from opening one and trying it." "I can imagine," said Emily "What was it like?"

"It's what you're chewing now," said Adam.

"The chew!" said Emily suddenly concerned about what she had done. "Yes, but don't worry Emily, the damage has already been done." Never the less, Emily felt uncomfortable with the chew in her mouth so she spat it out into her hand and squeezed it thinking of how it had been forbidden by God. Then she asked,

"So why has the garden been damaged by chewing the chew?"

Adam started to dig his hoe into the soil around the bottom of the fruit tree with the bad bark and answered,

"Good question Emily. We had to ask God that and he told us that everything in the garden was linked to everything inside of us. God explained that, just like the chew that we can make bubbles with, we have feelings inside of us called 'desires' which can grow inside us just like a bubble. When these 'bubbles of desire' grow a lot they squash everything else inside of us. The 'bubble of desire' inside of us can take over us." Adam took a handful of straw from a wheelbarrow and began to mix it into the soil with his hoe hoping to give the tree some extra food.

Emily replied, "So when we have times when we just really want something and we can't think of anything else, that's the bubble of desire getting big in us and squashing everything else down in us?" "Yes," said Adam "It squashes out your manners and your kind words and all sorts of things that make you a nice person. It turns out the 'bubble of desire' inside of us also damaged the water in the garden." Adam picked up a brown clay watering pot and the water sprinkled out of the bottom of it onto the trunk of the fruit tree. "Is that the water from the fountain coming out of the stone carved swans?" asked Emily

"Yes, that's our water supply and it turned bitter from the day we chewed the chew," said Adam thumping his hoe into the soil.

"You mean, the day your 'bubble of desire' got too big?" Adam then looked at the bird straight in the eye as he replied "Yes, that's right, the day our bubble of desire got too big, so big in fact that it ruined our garden."

"Couldn't God fix it for you?" asked Emily hopefully. There was an awkward silence and Emily could tell her question had made Adam feel emotional because his eyes clearly filled up with tears. "Seems like the bubble of desire even squashed our friendship with God," said Adam with a tremor in his voice –"God couldn't trust us anymore."

"I'm so sorry," said Emily, showing she cared about Adam's feelings. "We're the ones who need to be sorry," said Adam. "After all, we've changed everything now."

"Oh dear," said Emily, wondering what else she could say. "Is there nothing that can be done?"

"No," said Adam. "We've got to accept the consequences. The chew, or 'bubble gum' as you so nicely call it, is the perfect way to remember our lesson –the lesson that our desires can grow like bubbles inside of us and boy do we need to be more careful about that!"

"Wow!" said Emily "so this is how it all began in the beginning." "Mmm," murmured Adam not really understanding what Emily was saying or how much Emily knew about the future. "Adam, it's been so lovely to meet you," said Emily suddenly thinking she had lost track of time and it was probably time for her to be getting back.

"And you, Emily" replied Adam. "Oh, one thing you should know if you're visiting, is beware of the talking Galah [*gulaa*]," and as Adam pointed to the bird sitting on the spade handle it arched its wings and hissed at Emily.

"Oh?" said Emily remembering the swooping encounter she had had earlier.

"He knows how to make trouble," said Adam.

"Oh right, thanks Adam," replied Emily wondering if that meant the rose pink Galah had had a role to play in Adam eating the chew. "Hopefully see you again soon," and with that she waved and headed off to follow

her footsteps through the garden and back to the Ticking Box. But as she went through the trees and around in the direction of the stone steps the Galah appeared again, hovering just above her shoulder. Emily was able to see him quite clearly now. His feathers were as smooth as silk and he had some impressive head feathers that looked a bit like a feathered crown. His beak was black and looked as sharp as slate and it scared Emily a bit to think of what he could do with it. The Galah began to speak.

"You should mind your own business young lady," he said in a surprisingly clear voice which sounded a bit sly. Emily ignored the bird.

"You're a bit of a nobody young lady. You don't really belong anywhere and you certainly don't belong here, sticking your nose in to others people's gardens." Emily kept silent but the Galah's words hurt her. It was true, she had spent all her life moving to new places and being the new kid! And whilst she did make friends, she also seemed to make enemies too, of girls that didn't want her around or upsetting the balance of different groups of friends. She had often been told she was not welcome and did not belong, and Emily had had to get used to it. Why did the Galah choose to use those very familiar words with her? Adam was right, the Galah was trouble and he was causing Emily trouble right now, bringing up those unhappy feelings and memories for Emily and making Emily feel she was not welcome on this visit. "I know your secret," continued the bird. "I know you came here with the Ticking Box." Emily looked at the Galah straight in the eyes wondering why he seemed to be building up to threaten her. The bird continued, "Just remember young girl, I'm in control around here so don't think you can come and go as you please."

"Goodness, you're an unpleasant control freak," thought Emily, although she dared not speak it out loud to the Galah. Maybe he knew what she was thinking, because at that moment he flew off and out of sight and Emily was pleased to find the safety of the Ticking Box. She didn't usually tell anyone about when others had been unkind to her and so it didn't occur to her to tell the Ticking Box about the Galah.

Instead, Emily couldn't stop thinking about meeting Adam, and seeing the dying garden and she was desperate to ask what could be done about the bubble of desire. After all, it seemed as though all the problems in all the world seem to be caused by the 'bubble of desire'. The kind voice of the Ticking Box agreed that we could all do with the ability to look inside ourselves to understand our desires. Then the kind voice congratulated Emily on making a very wise decision about coming to meet Adam and said that she had passed the test and could be trusted to continue the adventure if she would like to. If you would like to know what Emily did next, read on.

4. DISCOVERING JOSEPH

The Ticking Box congratulated Emily on making the wise decision of visiting Adam. The kind voice said that it showed Emily had good character and she could be trusted to continue the adventure and make some more trips. The kind voice also reminded Emily that she had all the time *in time* for this adventure and she didn't need to worry about being late for school. Emily still didn't think about asking how she would get home. Instead she realised that she wanted more than anything to find out about whether Adam's garden could be made well again and prevented from dying. At this moment, she wanted to continue her adventure, much more than going home and back to school.

Amazingly she had the chance, with the help of the Ticking Box, to actually find out the destiny of the garden. Maybe, just maybe she could help Adam.

When the Ticking Box asked where Emily would like to go next, she remembered she had been singing in a school play called 'Joseph and his Multi-Coloured Dream Coat' and she knew that Joseph was one of the characters in the Bible. So she asked to visit him.

With the help of the kind voice, Emily turned the dial around and placed her hands on the Ticking Box and within a few moments it had brought Emily through another space wormhole and into a different garden. This one was hot and there were people pouring water into enormous big flower pots which had large green ferns growing in them that created a small bit of shade. In the hazy distance, Emily could see the giant pyramids; she was in Egypt! The garden was mostly paved with stones and pretty picture mosaics made from lots of tiny coloured squares of stone. All the paths in this garden were straight with small stone walls at the edges. It seemed as though this was a cultivated little oasis surrounded by a hot desert. Emily followed the path, seeing something in the distance that drew her attention. As she got closer she could see what looked like giant cages and people sweeping them out with long handled brushes. As she got closer still she could see there were animals inside. Had Emily arrived at a zoo? She walked up to one of the cages and looked in. There were monkeys, some of them sitting scratching each other and a couple of other younger monkeys jumping around on a rope. They were very cute with bright beady eyes. The cage was huge, about as big as Emily's house, made from thick wooden beams and rope fencing. From the ceiling hung lots of thick ropes made from brown fibre twined together.

As Emily studied the monkeys, a man's voice shouted out to her,

“Young girl, pick up your brush and sweep!”

Emily looked around and saw a young man wearing a smart hat with a cotton drape hanging down the back and sides of it, presumably protecting him from the sun. The drape sparkled and looked to be covered in gold and bright coloured threads. The man, although he looked important and rich, seemed to be cleaning part of the cage. “Here you go,” said the man offering Emily a brush. Emily took it and, not wanting to create any problems, started to sweep. She brushed up some dirty straw enthusiastically and then leant on her brush to speak to the young man.

“I’m looking for Joseph,” said Emily with a strong clear voice. “Well, you’ve found him,” said the young man.

“You’re Joseph? With the multi-coloured dream coat and the eleven brothers?”

“Yes,” said Joseph with a puzzled face, wondering how Emily apparently knew so much. Emily remembered from her school play that Joseph had been bought as a slave by the Pharaoh, king of Egypt, and incredibly, through his skill of interpreting Pharaoh’s dreams, had been made Egypt’s Prime Minister.

“I thought you were Egypt’s leader?” enquired Emily, “and not a zoo keeper?"

"You, are well informed," said Joseph. "I am, indeed, Pharaoh's chosen leader and, like many Egyptians, I like to keep these monkeys as pets. My Mother always taught me as a child to take care of my pets by helping clean their cage. Even though I have servants, I take joy in caring for these friends of mine." Emily realised she was in the company of the real Joseph, and Joseph at the peak of his power, so she started sweeping as a sign of respect. Whilst she was sweeping straw and monkey droppings into a corner she could scarcely believe her eyes when she saw a familiar looking Galah sitting perfectly still on a bar in the cage! It looked as if it was asleep until one black glassy eye winked open and then shut again.

"I'm glad it's sleepy," thought Emily and she continued sweeping. "I didn't like the bird's stroppy behaviour last time." Just then there was a screeching of monkeys and Joseph began to shout at the monkeys and chase them around like a crazy man. The monkeys had taken Joseph's smart hat and were passing it around between them as if having a game. Joseph was obviously very annoyed and was jumping up and down trying to reach his hat which was being thrown around and was getting dirtier by the minute.

Eventually, one of the monkeys dropped it, and Joseph stamped on it before any other of the monkeys could get to it. "This is no way to treat your master!" scolded Joseph wagging his finger crossly at his monkeys. He picked up the hat which now had a large muddy footprint on it too, made up mostly of sludgey monkey droppings. Joseph did his best to clean it up by slapping it on his thigh and wiping it on his shirt and then put the hat back on his head. Emily giggled quietly, amused by the fact that Egypt's Prime Minister was wearing such a filthy hat because of his mischievous monkeys. Joseph now leant on his brush, apparently keeping an eye on Emily's efforts, whilst he peeled a small orange and handed a segment to one of the monkeys who had jumped onto Joseph's shoulder. "They love these oranges more than anything!" said Joseph.

"I can see," replied Emily looking up.

"But what they love, also traps them," continued Joseph.

“Oh?” said Emily, hoping Joseph would explain. Joseph turned to the wall and took hold of a rope with a coconut tied to the end of it. “This is our monkey trap,” explained Joseph.

“Really?” said Emily interested to hear how it worked. Joseph took another small orange from a barrel and then, opening the lid of the coconut, placed the orange inside before replacing the lid. He then hung the coconut by its rope up on a branch suspended in the cage. Before long, one of the monkeys had jumped across to it and put his hand through a small monkey hand sized hole in the coconut grabbing the orange. The monkey began to pull and shake it, with his hand still inside the coconut. Before long the monkey was beginning to squawk and tussle in annoyance with the coconut that would not give up its orange.

“You still cannot stop yourself after all this time!” Joseph chuckled.
“Poor thing,” said Emily sympathetically. “The hole is too small to get the orange out.”
“Clever girl!” said Joseph. “You are right, but the monkey wants the orange so much it will not let go and so my crazy little friend is trapped!” Joseph swung the rope with the coconut attached, and the monkey still holding on tightly, across to him and said, “and that, my dear girl, is how you trap a monkey!”

"That's simple," agreed Emily. "But why can't he learn not to do something that traps him?"

"A very good question. In fact a most excellent question," said Joseph smiling handsomely with his full lips. "It is the same reason why people get trapped by their strong desires."

"Really?" asked Emily, wondering what desires trap people.

"For sure," replied Joseph. "One day, after my time, my people will be treated badly in this country," sighed Joseph, looking into the distance as though he was having a day time dream "But, even though it will be better for them to leave Egypt, they will find it impossible to let go of the things they love in Egypt."

"Oh dear," said Emily sadly. "It's as though they need to come to their senses."

"You are wise," said Joseph. Emily smiled back in appreciation. "They must come to their senses and learn to avoid the things that trap them; their lives will not be made better but worse by such things. This is the beginning of wisdom." Wisdom, thought Emily, was a posh word for saying things that experience showed were true. Joseph was now feeding the frustrated monkey with orange pieces and it clearly had forgiven his master, wrapping its tail around Joseph's neck as though giving him a

hug.

"Where will your people go, do you think, when they leave Egypt?" asked Emily. Joseph looked distressed and murmured some words and groaned. He seemed to be seeing more in his day dream; perhaps he was thinking about how bad things would get in Egypt first. After a pause, he remembered Emily's question.

"When they leave Egypt?...Well, God has promised that he will take us to a garden flowing with milk and honey."

"A garden!" exclaimed Emily excitedly. "God's taking you back to the garden."

“Yes,” said Joseph, surprised by Emily’s excitement. “My Great Grandfather heard God promise him that he would give us a garden and we’ve been waiting to see how that will come about. We know we haven’t got there yet.”

“You have dreams don’t you?” said Emily boldly.

“Yes,” said Joseph “and they’re not always good dreams. But they always come true.”

“I know,” said Emily, remembering the story from her school play about Joseph.

“You do?” Joseph was confused about how one so young knew so much.

“I’m having a bit of one now,” continued Joseph.

“I thought so,” said Emily, “what do you see?”

“I see God taking my people out of Egypt into a desert where they will be hungry and thirsty for many years,” said Joseph.

“I know,” said Emily “it will be tough for you all.”

“Do you see too?” asked Joseph.

“Well, sort of,” said Emily, realising that, coming from the future, she had the gift of hindsight and history books!

“Although it will be tough, I think it will a time of learning, before we are allowed to go into the promised garden,” said Joseph thoughtfully.

“A time for growing up,” said Emily.

"Exactly," said Joseph, again amazed by Emily's wisdom. "Like the monkey needs to learn to avoid the orange trap, so my people will learn about avoiding the things that trap them, so that when they arrive in the garden they can enjoy it."

"That makes sense," said Emily "After all, that's where Adam and Eve went wrong. Their desires ended up becoming a trap that caused their garden to die."

"You too have heard about that garden?" asked Joseph.

"Oh yes!" said Emily thinking that surely everybody had heard that story.

"I must go and write all this down," said Joseph "It's been nice to talk to you young girl."

"I'm Emily," and she held out her hand.

"Nice to meet you Emily!" said Joseph, shaking it. And with that he put the monkey back on its branch and headed off up the path. Emily put her hand in the fruit barrel and thought she would stay for a few minutes to feed the monkeys before she too headed back. Their little faces were full of personality and Emily felt she could understand what they were saying just by looking at the expression in their big blue eyes. Just then, the rose pink Galah arched and flapped his wings and spoke up.

"Visiting time is over!" said the Galah in a voice that was becoming

familiar. He was very much awake now and Emily decided that this was the time to leave. She made her way to the thick wooden door of the cage and pushed it open. As she stepped through the doorway, the bird launched himself and swept passed Emily out through the door, scratching her face with the sharp talons on his feet as he went. "Oww!" cried Emily as she brushed her hair out of her eyes. The Galah circled back and spoke again

"Get in my way, and you may well get hurt!" The bird then flew off and out of sight and Emily, feeling a little shaken and upset and with her hand on her cheek, headed up the path and back to the Ticking Box.

When she found the Ticking Box, her scratch had started to bleed a little. The kind voice said how brave Emily had been facing the Galah but that she would have to prepare for more trouble. Again, Emily decided not to talk about the trouble with the Galah but wanted instead to talk more about how monkeys get trapped by their love of oranges. She realised that people have their traps too and remembered how she often said to her Dad to put his phone down and talk to her. Emily felt that the story about the monkey and the orange would help her Dad realise how he was trapped in a bad habit. The Ticking Box agreed and said that she would need to remind her Dad that he should just use his phone in his office from now on. This made Emily start to think about what life could be like if we were free from traps. And if you'd like to know where the Ticking Box took her next, then read on.

5. DISCOVERING DANIEL

Emily was interested to talk to the Ticking Box about what life could be like when people are free from traps and the kind voice encouraged her to make another trip. There would be more to learn about freedom from traps and also more news about the story of the garden. She decided that Daniel, which was her brother's name, would be a good person to visit, especially because she knew that the Daniel in the Bible was brave, facing the lion's den. Perhaps the encouragement to be brave with the pink Galah was in her mind too. Turning the bronze dial and placing her hands into the handprints on the Ticking Box, it was just a moment later when Emily arrived by the side of a river.

There were weeping willow trees on both sides of the river and a number of packs of geese wandering about. As Emily walked away from the Ticking Box, she could see a wooden boat house on the edge of the river with a wooden roof. Above its entrance hung a shield with a royal coat of arms which included a picture of a pink Galah. Emily braced herself as she approached it. Now inside, she could see some long thin rowing boats, some young men and women holding oars and moving around and some geese that were squawking and flapping in the boat house. As she peered in, a young man called out to her, "Cox –you're taking out Team One," and pointed to the boat on her left. Emily knew a cox was usually a smaller person who sat at one end of the boat and steered the boat and kept the rowers rowing in rhythm together. She could see the rowing boat and the team of young men and women who had already got themselves seated with their oars on the wooden pontoon decking keeping them steady in the water. There was one seat that was still empty, just where the cox would sit, so she made her way, bravely smiling at the crew as she went. As she got into the boat, she could see a goose sitting at the other end of the rowing boat. Emily looked puzzled as she took her seat and the young man facing her in the rowing boat noticed and commented

"Do you like our lucky mascot?"

"Yes, I suppose so," said Emily, unsure why the goose was there.

"It's only a tame one," said the young man. "It symbolises its wild cousin which can do such extraordinary flights."

"Oh, I see," said Emily.

"But Shelly, that's the goose's name, well all she's good for is lunch!"

"Really?" said Emily wondering why.

"Tame geese don't fly," said the young man, seeing Emily's confused face. "They give up their flights across the world when you feed them."

“Wow!” said Emily “They can really fly across the world?”

“Yes, and at great heights too. They’ve been seen flying over the highest mountains, six miles high!” The young man took hold of his oar with both hands. “And they work as a team like no other animal or bird.” He wrapped his oar against the pontoon decking “You going to start us off? The King’s Team Two are stealing a lead on us.” Emily could see the boat that had been next to them had already pushed off on their cox’s command, so Emily copied what she’d just heard the Team Two cox shout;

“King’s Boat One! On your marks, one, two and three,” and with that the rowers with their oars on the pontoon side gave a big heave. They pushed the boat away, and out through the boat house opening, that took them straight out on to the clear water of the river. Emily could hear the other cox shouting orders at her team so decided to give it a go herself.

“On my orders…Left one, two; Right one, two,” and to Emily’s amazement the rowers with their oars on her left side put their oars into the water and heaved and then the rowers on the right side repeated the action. Emily discovered there were two string cords, one either side of her and by pulling these she could adjust the rudder of the rowing boat and steer it quite easily. Off they went, down the river, the goose leaning its neck out of the front of the boat as if pointing the way.

As they got into a rhythm, she introduced herself. "I'm Emily."
"I'm Daniel," said the young man facing her, puffing for breath as he rowed. She couldn't believe how these meetings seemed to work out!
"Daniel, as in Daniel who was thrown into the lion's den?"
"Yes Emily. That was a scary episode," replied Daniel.
"Incredible!" said Emily, her eyes wide, she scanned him to look for any signs of claw marks. "You were so brave!"
"Thanks Emily, it wasn't easy when they told me I would be thrown into the lion's den if I carried on praying to God but I chose to trust God for my life and he came up trumps!"
"And now you are free to pray to God?" said Emily.
"Yes, in fact the King joins me now in my prayers to God because he believes too, after seeing me survive his lions."
"That's fantastic Daniel ! –Is this his boat?" asked Emily
"Yes, this is the King's rowing team – the best in Babylon." Emily thought they'd better both concentrate on their rowing now, especially if the King was watching, so she carefully plotted her boat's course. Her boat's team was strong and it wasn't long before they were overtaking the King's Team Two boat. It seemed like this was just a training session but the team of three girls and three boys were now dripping with

beads of sweat from their efforts. There were lots of tall, grand stone carved buildings on the edge of the river. Some of them had domed roofs with mosaic tiling that shone in the sunshine. Smartly dressed footmen stood by their entrances, busily escorting people around. Clearly Babylon was an important and wealthy city. As the boat glided under a rather elegantly carved stone bridge, Daniel spotted some geese taking flight.

"Watch Shelly!" said Daniel. Shelly, the goose at the front of the boat, had spotted the wild geese, which can fly, and which seemed to be starting a journey. Shelly began to honk loudly and flap her stubby wings. "She wants to join in with their great flight adventure to the other

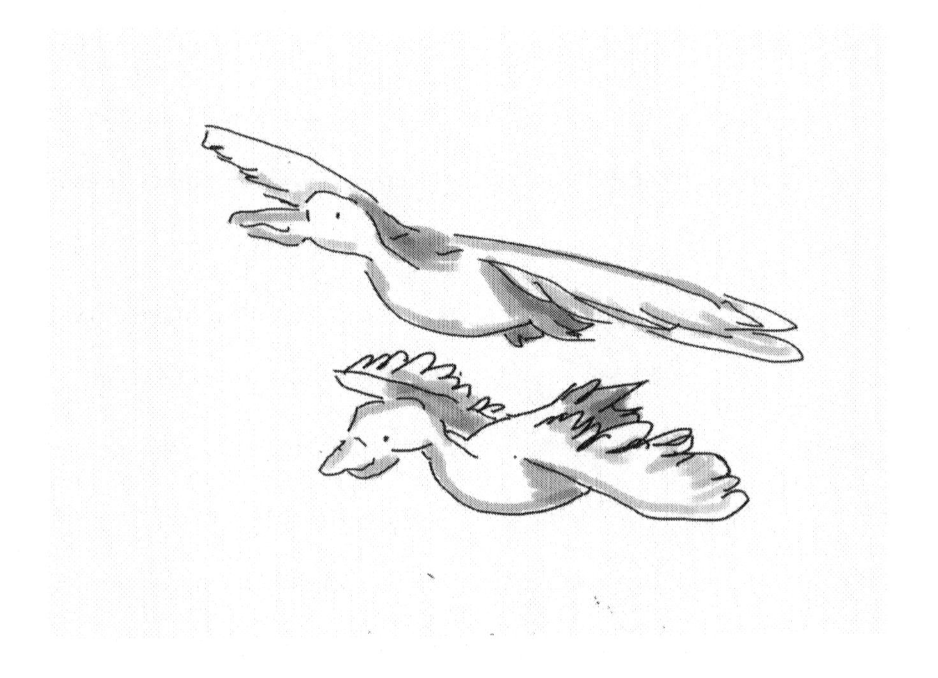

side of the world but she can't anymore," explained Daniel.

"Oh, how sad," said Emily sympathetically.

"It's her own fault," said Daniel. "She chose to accept the food people gave her and give up her amazing journeys."

"Looking at her honk and squawk , it's as though she's changed her mind," said Emily.

"Yes," said Daniel as he puffed out and pulled hard again on his oar. "Shelly has lost something and I think she knows it. The story of her life is not as glorious as her wild cousins." They rowed for what must have been an hour before they returned to the King's boat house. Shelly seemed to know she was back home judging by the way she squawked and strained her neck forwards and so she was unbuckled and let out first. Perhaps she was proud of her team because as soon as she was on the boat house decking, she strutted up to the rowers from King's Team Two and, wiggling her wings, started to peck the rowers' bottoms, much to the amusement of all the rowers. The King's Team Two rowers were giggling so much that they could hardly get away and ended up being an easy hopping target for Shelly as they tried to get out of the boat house. Once they had all finally got out and Shelly had calmed down, they sat down on the river's edge with their feet dangling in the cool water. A servant boy, about Emily's age, came and offered them all cool fruit drinks and broke up a small bread cake into small bits for Shelly as she stood expectantly with the rowers. But Shelly was to be disappointed because just as she stooped her long neck down to eat, a pink Galah swooped down and swallowed the bread pieces almost without breaking her flight. Shelly looked up hopefully, but the servant boy just shrugged his shoulders to say that he had no more.

"I see the pink Galah is being troublesome as usual," said Emily.

"Yes," replied the servant boy. "He can be a bit of a bully stealing Shelly's food." Shelly wandered off, pecking at the grass as a poor substitute.

"Why does the King's shield hanging on the boat house have a picture of the pink Galah on it?"

"Why do you think?" replied Daniel pointing to the Galah carrying off Shelly's bread. "Before the King believed in God, he trusted in his own strength that enabled him to bully people and steal from others in order to become rich and powerful. That's how Kings stay in charge."

Then Daniel stood up and addressed his rowing team and thanked Emily for being an excellent cox. She blushed with embarrassment only thinking how amazing it had been to have the opportunity. When he sat down, she thanked him for his words and then, pulling up some soft grass and throwing it towards Shelly the goose, she asked, “Why are you here in Babylon?”

“Well,” said Daniel sadly, “When my people left Egypt we eventually arrived in the Promised Garden flowing with milk and honey. But even though it was beautiful, we were greedy and we wanted more. So we gave up living the way God told us to live. People would cheat and betray each other; they would argue and fight and they failed to care for the poor. When the King of Babylon invaded our garden, we couldn’t work together as a team to fight him off. So he captured everybody and brought us here. The garden is a mess now and much of it was burned with fire.”

“It sounds like your people gave up their extraordinary living for tame goose living and they lost something,” said Emily thoughtfully.

“Yes, that’s very clever of you to see that similarity,” said Daniel. “When you become too selfish you lose something extraordinary.”

“You seem to have been able to be extraordinary,” said Emily thinking about the lion’s den.

“Well,” said Daniel, “I’ve been determined since a little boy to trust God and God has not let me down. In my dreams about God he promised to give me the gift to be extraordinary. He promised to give me the gift of courage.”

"Wow!" said Emily, "So perhaps that's why God has made you so successful in Babylon, so you can be an example and a good role model to your people and help them get free from the things that trap them."

"Gifts are to be shared I reckon," and Daniel winked. "It's funny we should talk about this Emily, because last night I had a dream where God said he would give this kind of gift to all his people when he sends his special King to lead the whole world to a new garden."

"Big wows!" said Emily. "God seems to be committed to sorting out his garden!"

"I think He is," said Daniel. "And to helping his people live like those extraordinary geese rather than tame ones – the two seem to go hand in hand." He stood up and pulled a warmer top on, "I'd better get back to the palace."

"I'd like to be courageous," said Emily thinking about Daniel's words.

"I think you already are," he replied. "I can see in your heart you are determined to stand for good not bad, and that path will always lead to conflict, where you will have to be brave and courageous." Daniel threw some bread he found in his pocket to some ducks that had swum close but they scattered as Shelley saw it floating and headed for it with a squawk and a large splash. "You see Emily, there will always be people who will give up the extraordinary and the good for an easier life."

Daniel patted Emily on the shoulder and walked off.

As Emily headed back up the path by the river towards the Ticking Box, she could see a flock of wild geese flying in the distance. They made two perfect lines forming a 'V' shape like an arrow head. As Emily watched the goose at the tip of the arrow shape, leading the way on their great journey, it touched her emotions and brought tears to her eyes. She knew Daniel was courageous and special but she couldn't stop thinking about the special one that Daniel believed would come in the future. He would be like the perfect wild goose and lead people into new courageous living and into a garden that would last forever. What would that be like? As Emily watched the Galah circling overhead, no doubt looking to steal food from someone else, she decided that, with the help of the Ticking Box, it was time to meet this perfect goose which she realised must be Jesus in the Bible, God in our shoes as they say, a real person. If you'd like to know about that adventure, read on.

6. DISCOVERING JESUS

Emily was beginning to realise that the garden involved some hard work. You could not neglect it if it was to grow well and be fruitful. And so far God's people had been learning a lot from their mistakes. She was far too interested in the story of the garden now to think about going home and so she spoke to the Ticking Box. Emily wanted to meet Jesus, who Daniel had believed would sort out the problems with the garden and God's people. As she moved the dial and held the Ticking Box, she could hear a quiet whirr of the layers of spheres as she began to move towards the opening mouth of a wormhole tunnel. What seemed like

seconds later, Emily found herself arriving in a synagogue building, a Jewish place of worship. There were lots of children of different ages and one of them was being carried through to the front of the room by some men. They were speaking an ancient language which Emily couldn't understand, but everybody seemed happy. There were bursts of applause for the boy every so often and he beamed with a great big wide smile. He was asked to read a few words from a scroll opened up in front of him and there was absolute silence as he read. Then, the scroll was rolled up, and everyone broke into applause again and there was celebratory singing and dancing in the big square room. It looked a lot of fun and Emily thought the boy must be having a birthday except there were no balloons or happy birthday signs hanging up and no sign of presents. Very soon the children were grouped together and a thin athletic looking woman with curly blonde hair led them off out of the room, through a foyer entrance and down some steps. As Emily followed, caught up in the crowd, she could see they were heading down a narrow side alley street made of cobble stones. As she walked, looking at the shops and houses on either side of the narrow street with their pretty clay roof tiles, she felt something large hit her on the head. It made quite a thud before breaking into bits as it hit the cobbled stone floor. It gave Emily such a shock that she yelped! Everybody turned around to look at her, which made her blush, before another missile landed just to the side of her. The party boy pointed to the pink Galah sitting on the edge of the roof top, overhanging the narrow street. "Watch out!" he said "The Galah is bombing you!" and with that he ran into one of the shops. Emily wondered if he was hiding as she kept her eye on the Galah who had another ball in his claws, waiting for his moment. The party boy re-appeared with a string and something attached to it. He started swinging it above his head and the Galah launched itself off the roof and dived down to the treat on the end of the rope which he caught with his talon claws and then landed smartly to peck and chew his treat. The party boy then swiftly grabbed the Galah and walked across to Emily.

"Here's your villain!" said the boy. "The pink Galah!" he exclaimed. "Unbelievable!" whispered Emily smiling at the boy "This bird keeps trying to get me!"

"Here, hold him by his legs!" he said, offering Emily the Galah. Emily was quite scared now. She was actually touching her enemy! But she felt she had to go along with the offer. As she held the Galah's legs tightly together with both hands, the boy firmly grabbed one wing, pulled it out so it was spread open and quickly clipped its large wing feathers until they were about half their original length. "That should humble

you!" he said as he repeated his feather cutting on the other wing and, taking the bird from Emily, he put him down on the cobbled stones. The Galah flapped his wings vigorously but it was no good. With his wing feathers clipped he could not fly. He could only jump up and down like a rather comical clown. The boy turned to Emily and explained that the pink Galah had always been violent with people and clipping its wings was always the best way to reduce the damage the Galah could do, so that it couldn't drop things from the sky.

Emily thanked the boy and then asked "Is it your birthday?"

"No," said the boy. "It's my bar mitzvah."

"Oh of course," said Emily, remembering her school religious studies classes. "You're celebrating becoming a man in your culture."

"That's right," said the boy. "It gives me shivers to think it's my turn to do what thousands of my forefathers have done before me. It's a moment when every boy recognises he needs to take on some new responsibilities now he has become a man."

"I see," said Emily, wondering what that might involve, but her mind quickly moved on to where they might be going. "Is this walk part of your bar mitzvah celebration?"

"Sort of," said the boy. "One of the fun things to do in this town is to visit the underground caves."

"Oh really?" said Emily

"Yes, it's called Potholing and these caves are one of the great wonders of the world," said the boy "I hope you'll come and see."

"Right," said Emily a bit concerned about how dark and scary that might be. "I'm really here to look for someone called Jesus," she said wondering whether that might give her a way out of going underground.

"Pleased to meet you," said the boy.

"You're Jesus! And it's your bar mitzvah today?" Emily's eyes widened.

"Yes, why the surprise?"

"You're amazing!" said Emily and then realised she was reacting with her knowledge of the future.

"I'm thirteen!" said Jesus.

"I'm Emily," said Emily who now felt she had to go on the potholing trip. If this really was Jesus, she was with God in a human body, the Jesus most people went to church for in her world -she couldn't possibly miss out! Before long, the street which had houses on each side turned to a rock face, and the street became narrow. The sun was still quite high and cast its bright light on one side of the street leaving the other side in shadow. The athletic woman leading the group brought the line of children to a stop and began to speak. She motioned for Jesus to come forward to the front and then started to explain the tradition of this walk. Emily noticed the Galah was wandering around looking for food, when suddenly a cat pounced. Fortunately, the cat seemed to want to play rather than hunt, but the Galah squawked and pecked at the cat whilst running and hopping along. Life for the Galah would certainly be humbling for him now his greatest strength of flight had been taken away from him. Thankfully, this time, the cat seemed too hot or too old to be bothered carrying on the chase and the Galah rested behind some steps leading up to one of the walls in the rock face. "The bar mitzvah is a ceremony that marks a decision taken by Jewish boys 2,000 years ago, ever since our ancestor Abraham had his boys," explained the leader, putting her hand on Jesus' shoulder. "This decision is called a 'rite of passage' but it would be better to call it a 'responsibility of passage' because that is what our boys are doing. They are legally an adult and decide to take on the responsibilities of being a grown up of our community. They will go to war to protect us if necessary; they care for our community, especially the poor and the sick; they will also teach their families about God. This journey underground symbolises the process of growing up. Take, for example, the light and dark." The woman pointed to the sun shining on the rock face and the shadow on the other side of the street. "It is a reminder that we are made up of light which is good but we also have a shadow side which is not so good. When we grow up we must not keep our shadow side a secret." The woman looked at Jesus who smiled back and made a funny face as if to say he was scared of the shadow which made the woman chuckle and slap him gently on the cheek three times. But it made Emily think. Was *she* hiding things? Why did she prefer not to speak about the times when others were unkind to her? She had not felt like telling her parents that she was teased at school for not having a cool phone. Neither had she wanted to tell the Ticking Box about the unkindness of the pink Galah. She thought she would do later, but right now she wanted to hear more about the trip.

"And now we will start our journey of illumination," continued the woman. "We will go into the dark caves with our lights." With that, she turned and ushered the group through an arch in the rock face which opened up to a cave entrance. They needed to jump down a big drop which the woman helped everyone with and suddenly it was much cooler and damper and it was clear that the potholing trip had begun. There was a row of candles in candle holders which everybody helped themselves to and then lit. The cave lit up a warm browny yellow. "You will need to stay close to the person in front of you and listen for my words. And everyone, you will need to make yourself small to get yourself through the bar mitzvah passages." They started to walk down a small corridor in the rock which gradually became smaller and smaller until everybody was on their hands and knees. Emily didn't feel too confident, especially because she was at the back, but she tried to take comfort by the fact she was not alone. After a few more metres, Emily needed to follow the others in front of her and lie on her tummy and pull herself along by her arms. The floor was quite smooth so she could slide her candle holder along the floor in front of her and then move forward metre by metre. Before too long she could hear the children talking and she realised she was coming out into a more open space. As she picked herself up off the ground she looked around. It was a big cavern with long tall columns. They were stalagmites which had grown all the way up to the ceiling. Some were narrow enough to get your arms around, but some were huge and would take five or ten people to link arms around one and Emily wondered how old they were. She guessed they were probably older than her tower but not as old as the Ticking Box.

"Now, if any of you have bags, you must leave them here –they'll be quite safe but there is no room for them on the Journey of Illumination. You will get stuck in the tunnels and need to be rescued. And this, my friends, is a message of the bar mitzvah: Through life you need to be willing to let go of many things in order to complete the journey." Emily began to think what that might mean but was interrupted by the woman's voice saying, "Keep walking," which echoed over and over again as it bounced around the cave walls. Jesus was counting people through and slapping them on the back affectionately with a smile.

"And now you Emily," said Jesus and he tilted his head and pointed the way forward for her.

"Why are you at the back?"

"Being a grown up is about putting others before you," he whispered.

"I see! Thanks," replied Emily. Over the next hour or so they went through a variety of caves and tunnels of different shapes and sizes and Emily enjoyed hearing about Jesus' brothers and friends at school and the things they did. She also talked to Jesus about Adam's garden that was dying and Joseph's dream about needing to be prepared for a new garden and Daniel's sadness that their garden hadn't lasted and how God would send someone perfect to finally lead people into a new garden. Jesus listened carefully but didn't have much to say. One of the caves had a cool stream running in it and they were all able to have a refreshing drink, scooping up the water with their hands and gulping it down. That was especially nice as crawling around underground so much was hot and dusty work. The caves were all rather amazing to see, but Emily was quite tired now and one cave seemed to be very much like the rest from her point of view. She was a bit relieved when the woman leader, who was called Zea, announced that they were now heading for the final tunnel leading to the final cave.

"The final tunnel is extremely tight and you will need to take your time..but it's worth it!" said Zea enthusiastically. The group made their way, one by one, until it was Emily's turn. She stood looking at the extremely small tunnel and suddenly felt scared. She had been mostly okay so far, but now the thought of getting stuck and not being able to breathe and never being able to get out suddenly filled her with dread. She took a step backwards and began to shake.

"I know, Emily," said Jesus calmly, "anxious feelings can make you quite wobbly," and he encouraged her to sit down.

"I'm not sure I can go through," she said with a catch in her throat. Jesus sat down next to her. He was much bigger than Emily, being four years older and obviously having gone through a bit of a growth-spurt. "It would be such a shame not to make it through to the final cavern," said Jesus "it's supposed to be the best of all and I'm excited we're going to see it today."

"I know, but I feel so scared now." She held her hand out and watched it

tremble.

“What’s your biggest fear?” asked Jesus

“I think it’s getting so stuck that I won’t be able to breathe.”

“Emily, I want you to wait here whilst I go through,” said Jesus. “Don’t worry, I won’t leave you here.” And with that, Jesus scrambled down on to his tummy, and twisted and contorted his large thirteen year old body through the tiny dark tunnel. Emily could hear gravel falling off the tunnel walls as he went until there was silence and just her small faint candle lighting up the space in front of her. In the lonely quiet of the cavern, she studied the rock formations on the tunnel entrance looking at the stripes in the rock that made up its layers. She didn’t want to be stuck here at this moment and thought about how she wanted to be safe at home. As she was running her hand across the stripey rock the silence was broken. She heard Jesus’ voice. “Emily, Emily, you’ve got to come through! It’s the most beautiful cave you will ever see!” At that moment, Emily found the confidence to make her way through the tunnel. It was as though someone had turned on the taps inside of her and now she was being filled up with courage. Hearing Jesus’ voice changed everything. If Jesus, who was bigger than her, could do it, then so could she. She slid down on her tummy and edged her way forward, boldly squeezing her body to each nook and cranny as she went. It hardly seemed like any time at all before she saw the light from the final cavern and Jesus' hand stretched out to help her up. She was through! She hugged Jesus with delight.

"Your words from the other side made all the difference to me," said Emily. As she looked around she was amazed by the brightness of this cave. The cave was full of crystals -the colours were extraordinary, dark blues fading to light blues, pure white, deep reds fading to pinks. It was as though the crystal magnified several times the light from everybody's candles. The cave was mesmerizing!

"It's beautiful," said Emily turning around and around, slowly trying to take it all in.

"Worth the scramble wasn't it?" said Jesus

"I'm so glad I made it," replied Emily. "I'll never forget it." Zea then began to explain that this last passage, into the glorious bright final cavern, symbolised our lives. The final tunnel everybody has to face is the time when we die and then pass on to a new life in heaven with a perfect new body. This final cave, that glitters and sparkles, represents the new heaven, that God will make visible on the earth, where the city and the garden will be restored.

"Jesus, the garden is going to be made well again!" exclaimed Emily. But Jesus was silent, looking at the crystal. "What are you thinking?"

she asked.

“I’ve realised what the bar mitzvah means for me,” replied Jesus.

“You mean, what you have to do as a grown up?”

“Yes Emily, I think I know that my job is to be courageous and go first so I can speak to you from the other side of the final tunnel,” he said calmly.

“Do you mean be a guide on potholing trips?” said Emily uncertain what Jesus meant.

“Sort of,” said Jesus, and he pointed the way for Emily to follow the others as they headed for the way out of the caverns and back to the synagogue where they had come from.

On the way, Emily saw the pink Galah trying to get some scraps from a spilt rubbish bin, but he was in competition with some dogs who pushed and butted him out of the way. The Galah had to wait its turn and was already looking tired and a bit shabby from life on the ground. Emily felt sorry for the Galah, but she was beginning to understand that rejecting responsibilities for thinking about others had consequences for everyone. She hoped the Galah might realise that too.

When Emily got back to the Ticking Box at the synagogue where she had left it, she wanted to ask it one question. “Jesus meant he would be the first to speak to us from the other side of dying didn’t he?” she said. “That was the final tunnel he meant.”

“Yes,” said the kind voice, “He is the first in the new garden.” Emily smiled knowing she wanted to see that garden and if you’d like to know about that adventure, read on.

7. DISCOVERING HERTH

Meeting Jesus had changed things for Emily and it seemed to her that every day would now be different because of it. She now knew that being born in this world was only the first part to life. There was a new life to come after this life and if that wasn't enough to be excited about, the garden was now going to be made well, presumably forever. "How wonderful," thought Emily. "It makes me think 'what are we waiting for?'" she said to the Ticking Box.

"Perhaps you'd like to get some sight of the future?" said the kind voice "And make a brief journey to this new garden."

"I'd love that!" replied Emily and so she followed the instructions of the Ticking Box and before she knew it she was coming out of another wormhole tunnel into a park where there was a big adventure playground made of wood and coloured ropes and platforms in the trees with rope bridges.

There were picnic tables and barbeques mounted on stone blocks. The sun was shining through tall trees with fresh green leaves and it was warm. There were lots of colourful small parakeets in the trees chirping away and there were bear cubs wandering around the picnic area, digging around the bottom of the trees as though they were looking for honey or something sweet. As Emily looked around she could see a young man cooking on one of the barbeques. She walked towards him and he looked up and smiled.

"Hello," he said warmly, "I'm Ben."

"Hello Ben, I'm Emily," and she put out her hand which he shook. "So this is the new garden?" said Emily.

"Part of it," said Ben.

"And are things growing well in the garden?" she asked anxiously. "Never better!" said Ben smiling and putting what looked like chopped sausages into two pitta breads.

"Wow! So God really has restored the garden."

"Yes, and the city," said Ben.

"Oh great," said Emily, not quite knowing what that meant. "I don't see the city?" she continued.

"It's all around us," said Ben. "You're in it!"

"So, the city is a garden?" asked Emily

"And the garden is a city," replied Ben.

"So where do people live?"

"I'll show you," replied Ben and he offered Emily one of the pitta breads and then took a big satisfying bite out of his. It smelt good so Emily tried some. It was delicious. One of the bear cubs had made its way over and Ben put his hand out with a small bit of the pitta bread. The bear licked it off his hand and it was clearly so delicious to him that he wanted more and jumped up on his hind legs to ask. Unfortunately, it knocked Ben backwards and before Emily had time to worry whether he was hurt from the fall or even might get hurt by the bears, the bear started licking Ben's face. Ben burst into giggles and cuddled the bear

cub and they rolled over and over. The bear cub seemed to know his wet tongue tickled Ben and he kept coming back to lick him again. Ben was in fits of giggles and he seemed to quite forget that Emily was with him. Emily thought it was a lovely sight to see boy and animal enjoying each other so much. Eventually, Ben gathered himself and patted the bear and smiled at Emily.

“He’s so friendly,” said Emily, realising that normally she’d be a lot more anxious about a bear being so close.

“Yes,” said Ben as he led her along a path through the park. “Everything in Herth is friendly.”

“Herth?” questioned Emily. “Is that what this place is called?”

“Yes,” said Ben “God added the ‘H’ to earth, just like he added the ‘H’ to Abram to make him AbraHam. It reminds us that we’ve all agreed God is now in charge. And of course, Herth is the place where God is now visible.”

“I think I want to come and live here now,” said Emily “It’s so beautiful.”

“Yes,” said Ben, “it truly is paradise.”

They were now walking through a colourful walled garden in which bees were busy at work flying between the flowers, and two rabbits were skipping around playfully. Ben opened a wooden door, which had been painted royal blue a long time ago and looked as soft as linen. They stepped through, out of the walled garden and on to a gravel drive. There, before them, was a big house made from large golden sandstone bricks. There were big windows in the house with elegant thick curtains hanging from them.

“Is this where you live?” asked Emily.

“Yes,” said Ben. “We live together as a family again.”

“Oh?” said Emily enquiringly.

“It’s part of God’s plan for restoration,” said Ben. “God has made people in families, happy to be together again and it’s brilliant. We get to know all our great great great grandparents!”

“Wow!” said Emily, thinking that there would be a lot of catching up to do and how interesting it would be to hear the stories from everybody’s lives.

“And how do you get to the shops or to see other people?” asked Emily. “Have you got cars?”

“Sort of,” said Ben. “We’ve got something even better called the ‘Ticking Box’.“ Emily smiled. “It might sound strange,” continued Ben “but it’s this incredible box that you put your hands on and then you go anywhere you want to go.”

“Incredible!” said Emily, not letting on that she had already had plenty of experience with the Ticking Box. “So it’s a happy ending.” “Well, we love what God has done with Herth,” said Ben, “but so many of us wish we’d done more to prepare for Herth.”

“What do you mean?”

“Well, the last Earth was the raw material for ‘Herth’,” explained Ben. “It was as though Earth was used as the clay to make a new pot, or to put it another way, the seed that grew into a new plant.”

“Oh, I see,” said Emily. “So somehow, what we do on earth, has an effect on what God does on Herth.”

“Exactly,” said Ben. “So, those bears you saw, were made new again from some orphan bear cubs on Earth that the Rangers at Yosemite Park in America looked after and protected from hunters.”

“Wow!” said Emily.

“Everything here has its connection with Earth,” explained Ben.

“What, even the food?”

“Well, the food depends on the soil,” said Ben, “and God couldn’t use a lot of the soil on earth because it was so polluted. Our food comes from the good soil that God was able to use on Earth to make new soil on Herth.”

“Oh, I see.” Emily thought for a moment and remembered the water that turned bitter in Adam’s garden. “But how can we do anything on earth when the water is bitter?”

“Jesus sorted that,” said Ben. “He has given his people many gifts including turning bitter water into sweet water.”

“Wow!” said Emily “So our life on Earth is very important because it really is preparing things for this garden.”

“Yes, it certainly is,” replied Ben. This made Emily realise that she now couldn’t be in a rush to come to Herth. There was so much to do in her world – on Earth.

“What about our bodies on Herth?” asked Emily “They are restored too aren’t they?”

“Oh yes,” said Ben. “No more being ill or disabled – you live forever in perfect health here.” After a pause he spoke again “But you can tell who lived best on Earth because they look slightly older here."

"Oh?" enquired Emily.

"Yes, God says the invisible qualities in humans, such as love and hope and faith, he uses to make our new Herth bodies."

"Wow!" said Emily.

"Yes, and you can tell who those people are because they look at bit older and it seems natural to respect those who are older."

"And is Jesus here too?" asked Emily.

"Of course," said Ben. "God has made him King of Herth and he looks the oldest of all with his white hair and trendy beard. We call him the Ancient One, but that doesn't mean he's decrepit – no, he can move like the best of us!"

"That's great!" said Emily smiling at the thought of Jesus dancing. "One final question" said Emily inquisitively, "Do you know if the pink Galah is here in Herth?"

"Yeah" replied Ben "some of them?"

"What do you mean some of them? I thought there was only one?" said Emily.

"No, there were lots of them and God asked them if they wanted to live in Herth," replied Ben.

"What did they say?" asked Emily intrigued.

"Well, you know pink Galahs, they are pretty stubborn and bossy creatures who know their own mind. Some of them wanted to let Jesus rule and reign on Herth and some, as you can understand, really did not," explained Ben.

"So, the ones who wanted Jesus to rule and reign are here?" said Emily. Ben nodded. "And what happened to the ones who didn't want to stay on Herth?"

"Well," said Ben, "Jesus let them fly off but as they took off and circled upwards they turned into dust that looked like glitter and blew away on the wind."

"Wow!" said Emily "That's so sad that they didn't want to live here." "Well, we thought so too," replied Ben. "But Jesus said that our physical bodies are not ours. He only lent them to us and we have more than a lifetime to decide what we want to do when it's time to give them back." "So it's all our choice?" said Emily thinking about it. "Ben, it's been so lovely to meet you."

"And you too Emily."

"If you don't mind, I'll head back now," said Emily realising it would take some time to work out what all this meant for her.

"You take care," said Ben and he put his hand on Emily's shoulder.

Emily smiled and then followed her footprints back to the Ticking Box. When she reached it, she sat down to enjoy a moment, taking it all in. She enjoyed the feeling of bubbly happiness knowing that her family, including her Grandad, would one day be re-united forever.
"I've learned a couple of things here," said Emily.
"Good," said the kind voice.
"Firstly, I have decided that becoming famous and having my own perfume or my face sold on T-shirts to make lots of money is a waste of time." The kind voice was silent. "Secondly, I have to get prepared for Herth and that means learning more about how to grow things on earth. I've to teach others about popping their bubbles of desire which damage the garden."
There was no reply again from the kind voice. Emily thought nothing of it, instead she knew she really wanted to go home now. The Ticking Box seemed to know, because Emily could hear the metal ball layers inside it whirring. She put her hands into the handprints and felt the gentle upward movement of the Ticking Box and the space ahead of her

funnelled into its final wormhole tunnel. Faster and faster it went, until things became so blurred Emily Grace could not make sense of what was around her. It was so overwhelming that Emily thought she must have passed out or fallen asleep.

The next thing she knew was being woken up for school by her Princess clock beeping its alarm at 7.30am. Emily would have almost got on with the day putting her amazing night down to a fanciful dream, but she couldn't. For one thing, well, it just seemed too real. And the second reason; her duvet was still lying half way across the bedroom floor where she had left it. "No, it wasn't a dream," she thought. Emily put on her school uniform, brushed her hair and set off downstairs to start the day.

Back at home, all this travelling had developed quite an interest for Emily in reading her Bible, especially about Adam, Joseph, Daniel and Jesus. When she got into bed on Friday night she read a verse that Jesus had said about God our Father in Herth. It read, "My Father is the gardener, he prunes every branch that bears fruit." "Wow!" thought Emily, "God is gardening us!" She looked at her clock and suddenly wondered if the Ticking Box was in fact God! After all, the kind voice had taught her so much about how to grow in her life. Emily thought it would be good to talk again to the Ticking Box, but as she picked up the clock to her surprise she found that the 'Receive' button had disappeared from the back of her clock. She ran to the window with her clock to see if the tower was glowing, but it wasn't. She lay back down again and wondered why there wasn't another invitation to go on an adventure. Putting her clock down on her bedside table, somehow she knew that the adventure with the Ticking Box was over. She turned on to her side looking at the second hand moving around. Tick, tick, tick, tick. As she watched, she was sure she could hear the words "so," tick, "I," tick, "am," tick, "with," tick, "you," tick, "always," tick. From that day on, whenever Emily heard a ticking clock, she heard those words in her head: "So-I-am-with-you-always." And those words always helped Emily to be brave and courageous and the little things that had bothered her before, like friends being mean or a house that wasn't as nice as Emily would have liked, seemed to become less and less important. Now, there was something so much more important to be concerned with.

If you are wondering what Emily decided to do now the Ticking Box adventure was over I'll tell you. Emily's first actions were to plant some seeds with her Grandma who had come to visit. It was Spring and a good time for planting and her Grandma could teach her all sorts of things about planting. Then, on a trip to the local park, there was a petition to sign to save the butterfly house from being closed down. Emily signed it and added a note saying that she'd be happy to volunteer in the butterfly house if there were any jobs that needed doing. While in the park, she picked up some litter for a few minutes before having a go on a swing. As she swung her legs to get the swing moving, she gazed at her tower in the distance, looking at all its thousands of bricks. She thought how much time it must have taken to make each one and then lay them row by row. "That's it!" she thought, "by doing acts of kindness and love I am building a tower of bricks for Herth." Life for Emily would now always be

different.

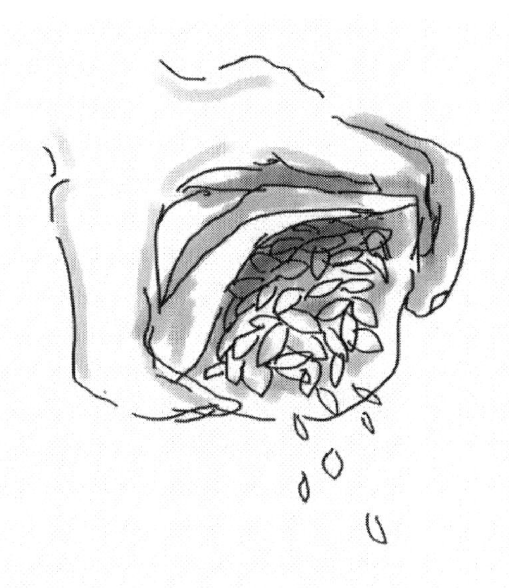

If you have enjoyed Emily's story why not follow @TickingBoxStory on Twitter and share with others #bricksforherth.

ABOUT THE AUTHOR

Mark Cowling is married to Rachel and they have three young children who patiently sit through his stories. Since being a boy, when his father made up stories about Woof Woof at bath time and bedtime, Mark has enjoyed writing stories himself. Mark currently works for the Church of England and has woven some of his teaching illustrations into this journey with the Ticking Box.

Made in the USA
Charleston, SC
07 March 2016